MW00532585

MIGRAINE
AND MIA

By Kat Harrison

Illustrated by
Marusha Belle

Copyright © 2021 by Kat Harrison. All rights reserved. This book may not be reproduced or stored in whole or in part by any means without the written permission of the author except for brief quotations for the purpose of review.

ISBN: 978-1-954614-35-2 (hard cover)
    978-1-954614-36-9 (soft cover)

Editing: Amy Ashby

Published by Warren Publishing
Charlotte, NC
www.warrenpublishing.net
Printed in the United States

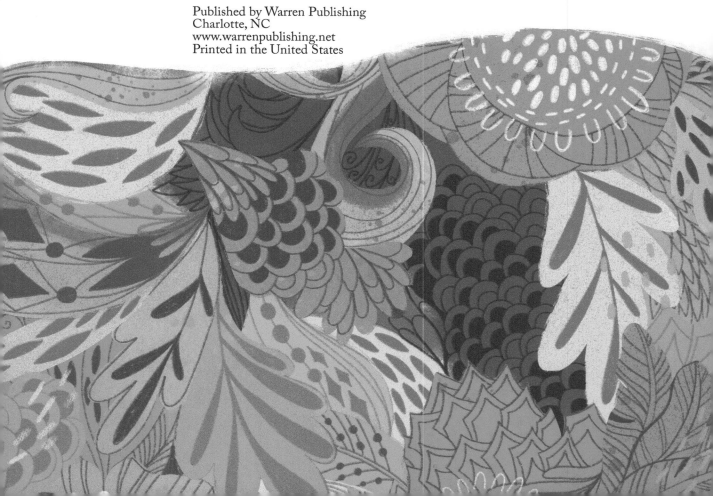

To Mike –
For the hundreds of cozy caves you've built me.

and

To Ryan –
For all of the small (and thoughtful) ways you help.

Hi, I'm Mia and I have chronic migraine.
Have you ever had one?
They're the opposite of fun.

You see, a migraine isn't just a headache.
It's a full-body pain parade
that'll make your stomach swashbuckle
and your skin swelter.

For some,
it can feel like a marching band behind your eyeballs,
getting struck by a lightning bolt,
or wearing a too-tight helmet to bed.

Sometimes it might feel like
your brain has been turned to scrambled eggs.
It can be hard to think,
or speak,
or even laugh at really funny jokes.

And a migraine can sneak up on you—it's true!
In the morning,
night,
or in the middle of biting into the world's best donut.
(And I do love donuts.)

Imagine:
a puppy pawing into your cheeks,

a prickly cactus playing hopscotch on your skin,

or a mouth full of cavities! Yikes!

A migraine can make you see dots,
or stripes,
or turn your vision into a color-changing chameleon.
(Doctors call that an aura.
Some call it art. I call it gross.)

Light of all kinds can hurt and make a migraine grow.
They're bothered by yucky weather too—
falling rain or sticky air—
like a weather vane for brain pain.

DiNG
DONG

A migraine can sound like
a rapid heartbeat with the volume turned up,
or a ringing bell held right up to your ear.

It can hate the smell of stinky cheese,

p-p-puffs of perfume,

or the stench of bug spray.

So, if you meet someone with a migraine,
build them a comfy and cozy cave—

fluff up their pillows,

turn off the lights,

pour them a glass of water just right,

and then leave quietly like a mouse.

Because tomorrow is a brand-new day!

Did you know?

- One in ten children has migraine. That means if there are twenty kids in your class, it's likely that two of them live with migraine.

- Migraine affects over 1 billion people worldwide.

- Over 39 million men, women, and children in the US live with migraine.

- One in four households in the US has a member with migraine.

  Migraine is a very difficult disease to live with because it hurts and gets in the way of school and hobbies. But migraine is also invisible, so friends and family might not know if you live with it. That is why it is so important to talk about migraine and teach people that it's more than just a headache.

You are not alone.

Visit the American Migraine Foundation's Pediatric Migraine Hub for more resources designed to help children and families living with migraine. The hub features articles about healthy habits, guides to requesting accommodations in schools, and more. https://bit.ly/amf-migraine-kids

The American Migraine Foundation (AMF) provides useful doctor-verified resources for people living with migraine and their caregivers. The opinions and content in this book are not written by or with the AMF, and are not endorsed by the AMF.

CPSIA information can be obtained
at www.ICGtesting.com
Printed in the USA
LVHW070830231021
701271LV00003B/27

9 781954 614352